Josephine

A pathway to freedom

Virginia Elena Patrone

dixi
books

The Voice of the New Age

Josephine: A Pathway to Freedom
Virginia Elena Patrone
Editor: AJ Collins
Proofreading: Andrea Bailey
Designer: Pablo Ulyanov
Cover Design: Virginia Elena Patrone

Printed in Bulgaria
I. Edition: May 2018

Library of Congress Cataloging-in- Publication Data
Elena Patrone, Virginia, 1985.
Josephine - A Pathway to Freedom/Virginia Elena Patrone. - 1st ed.
ISBN: 978-619-90997-4-2
1. Fiction 2. Literature Fiction

© Dixi Books Publishing OOD
9, Pozitano Str. Ent. B, Fl 1, Office 2, 1000, Sofia, Bulgaria
Bambergstr. 21, 59192, Bergkamen, Germany
info@dixibooks.com

Josephine

"If she's real, we say she's trying to be a man
While putting her down we pretend that she is above us"
~John Lennon, Woman is the nigger of the world

"But almost without exception they [women] are shown in their
relation to men. It was strange to think that all the great women of
fiction were, until Jane Austen's day, not only seen by the other sex,
but seen only in relation to the other sex. And how small a part of a
woman's life is that; and how little can a man know even of that when
he observes it through the black or rosy spectacles which sex puts
upon his nose."
~Virginia Woolf, A room of one's own

"O, wonder!
How many goodly creatures are there here!
How beauteous mankind is!
~William Shakespeare, The tempest

Preface to the book

The energies of the universe and the need to be free

In the universe exist many types of energies, some of which take shape on the Earth and form what we call the world. Two of these energies are the female and male: the reason we are biologically born – human, plants and animals – either as female or male or as both. This does not mean that any one female is the exemplification of the female energy of the universe, nor that one male can represent all males, because these energies can form differently within each person; therefore, a female can feel more male and vice versa. The energies have no sex. They are called male and female energies, but this is just a name. It is true that women are more likely to have a greater amount of female energy, and men a greater amount of male energy. But this is not mathematical.

For the same reason, our brain is divided into two parts: the right and left hemispheres. Each side works accordingly to one of two energies: the left hemisphere is associated with logic, rationality, subdivision and organisation of things, and hierarchy and perpetuation of the status quo. The right hemisphere is intuitive, imaginative and unconventional, but does not perceive edges[1] – boundaries of the past. Rather, it perceives the colour of things, which is the pure essence of life. It is innovative, non-competitive, and it communicates without words – language that belongs

---

1 Borders are the limits of the past and the contours of our existence. They are the edges of the objects we have not yet imagined, and those we have already encountered. They are the laws, the conventions and rules of good manners, which we adopt to allow us to live within a community.

to the left brain, where there are limits[2]. The right brain has the ability to have a unified view of the whole, and can easily accept diversity, because everything is the expression of the same being. For this reason, the right side of our brain also represents our connection to the divine.

Everything that happens in the world, and in our lives, can be seen as a metaphor. There is a bigger reason, a higher and mythological cause for facts and events to happen.

In our current patriarchal society, the part of the brain that works most is the left side: technology, logic, and rationality are often considered superior to intuition, artistic spirit and imagination. People who are guided by the "female" energy – the right hemisphere – about choices, work, schooling, or any other aspect of life, are often affected by the impossibility of expressing themselves, because what they do or say is not taken into account, as it is often regarded as being of little value. Take for example the creative category of artists, painters and writers: we see they are far outnumbered by the technical category of engineers, builders, architects, lawyers, doctors and so on. Not to mention that most artists who are considered successful are those who have benefitted financially from their art, becoming caught up in a competitive and hierarchical circuit, rather than being appreciated purely for their artistic talent and self-expression – something that cannot be measured in terms of money.

Art must be free and cannot be hierarchised. Every artist is good in their own way, especially if during their life at home, at school, with friends and peers, they can scratch away the opaque patina represented by the conventions concealing their own vision of what does not yet exist, but which could exist in one of the myriad of possible futures. For this reason, art is divine: it is a window into one of those many possible futures.

---

2 Words themselves are already limits. A word says where a thing starts and where it ends. In addition, most languages have conventions, such as grammatical rules.

Regarding women, we cannot forget their position in today's society: women metaphorically represent that energy of the universe – the feminine – that our patriarchal society does not want to accept, and does not want to see, preferring to relegate, compress, erase. That is why, every day, acts of femicide are being perpetuated. Everywhere, around the world, a terrible number of women die, particularly at the hands of their husbands, fiancés, brothers. Women represent, metaphorically, the energy that also exists inside the executioners themselves – the one part they want to ignore because it reminds them they could be better than they are, if they could open up to a dialogue with that part of their being, instead of seeking inexorably to eliminate it.

Etymologically, the words matriarchal and patriarchal are derived from the ancient Greek word arché, which means domain. But in one of its most ancient synonyms, we find arché also means origin. (Göttner-Abendroth, 2013)

Then we understand that within the word patriarchal, arché assumes the meaning of domination: the dominion of the fathers. While for matriarchy, arché takes the sense of origin: the origin the mothers.

This not only emphasises that in the past, at the origins, most societies were primarily matriarchal, and only later became patriarchal, but above all, it denotes the idea that the mother is the origin of life. From a biological and social point of view, what this statement means is obvious, but it also has a very important metaphorical meaning: pregnancy is the only stage of human and animal life in which one being is physically one and two at the same time – the mother has her future inside herself, the child in her womb represents her plan to perpetuate herself in the world. By extension, every project that is an expression of the soul, is firstly formed as an idea that is given birth to, and needs to be nurtured and protected like a child. For each of these expressions are the perpetuation of that person, into the future world. So our children are metaphorically us, and when we are released from our past, we are born again as new people.

That's why it's important to free ourselves of our limited beliefs, to get rid of everything we know. For to imagine and accept whatever new is coming, we must first rid ourselves of inherited conventions and superstructures. To achieve this, we need to carefully look around each day and decide what we like and what we want to change.

Our daily actions lay the foundations for societies to come. Just ask the simplest questions – the ones children do when they are very young, when they still know everything about the world and about the universe, yet have no knowledge of the norms to be respected. A time when they constantly ask, "Why?" I guess very few adults will be able to answer these questions, and even truly free minded people will have difficulty explaining to children that some concepts can only be accepted, and have no explanation at all.

"Joséphine" is a short story that speaks of personal liberation. The tale is set in an unspecified time, since it tells the story of our ageless world. Joséphine is a young woman in the fullness of her youth, who was abandoned by her mother as a child, as often happens in fairy tales. This is not a random casualty: the fairy tales almost everyone knows – Snow White, Little Red Riding Hood, Cinderella, etc. – are reminders and evidence of the presence of matriarchal societies in ancient times, at least in Europe. It is true that the main characters of these tales are almost always female, but gender is not an important detail here because these stories speak about the liberation of the female energy that is inside every person, regardless of gender. The fact that the mother is always absent, denotes that the daughter is already the mother's transformation, the mother is the daughter because the daughter is the mother's evolution.

Don Diego represents the worst side of the status quo: the plotter and social climber, the unscrupulous individual whose personal condition can only be achieved by completely ignoring the condition of his brothers and sisters on this Earth. When the divine is forgotten.

To escape means to disengage from our past, to open ourselves to all the possibilities of happiness, or balance, we might find within us, once our transformation starts to take place. Of course, running away does not mean leaving our house, our city, or the country we are living in, to look elsewhere for what we want: in most cases, happiness is not a geographical condition, but something that grows or shrinks inside us. When we are happy, we feel that somehow our spirit becomes bigger, and we are better connected with that part of us which is timeless and immense – nowadays called "God".

On the other hand, when we are unhappy, we tend to be bound inside ourselves, our energy loses volume and we feel that something is wrong, but we do not know what: this means we are separated from our true spirit. Unhappiness, however, is not a state of mind to denigrate. On the contrary, it is a message that tells, or screams, to us that we must change, that we must look for something new: it is a state of potential, and if we can grasp this message, we have the opportunity to grow and expand.

"Joséphine" captures the theme of women living in patriarchal societies, across all ages and continents, relegated to their role of wives, mothers, and ghost like presences in homes where everything is expected to work effortlessly. It tells the story of a woman who has courage, and moves the mechanism of divine providence to save herself, and to create for herself a better future, in order to grow and evolve.

The patriarchal society invented the image of the chaste and submissive woman, and founded the myth of virginity: in practice this was the only way to know who really was the father of the children, as the Romans used to say: Mater semper certa est, pater numquam[3]. But Joséphine is a woman who discovers her sexuality, and refuses to forget that the body has needs that can be satisfied: needs of beauty within the physical world. Sexuality can and must be experienced with joy and cognition because it is in the ecstasy of orgasm that we lose contact with the world and time, and we are able to live in the infinite.

---

3 The mother is always certain, the father never.

For Joséphine, to fall in love is a metaphysical experience: it allows her to see her life from the outside – a metaphorical desert in which everything that was important to her has lost its value. Only then can she imagine for herself a bigger, wider future, because, from that moment, her spirit starts to occupy more space and she learns that there is no need to ask permission for what she already owns, or what she wishes to have.

Bibliography

Göttner-Abendroth, H. (2013). Le società matriarcali. Studi sulle culture indigene del mondo. Venexia.

Joséphine
Timeless Beauty

Last night, I dreamt of a soup tureen – one of those beauti-ful ones from Mason's: English, ceramic, white with a dark-pink image printed on it.

It was suspended in the air, alone with all its beauty, with nothing to distract it from my gaze. Magnetic, it drew my full at-tention on itself. Then my eye, now I recall, focused on the image on the tureen: a little girl who was holding her parents' hands and throwing some crumbs to a huge white swan.

After that, I dreamt of the old tureen's owner, a lord who kept it in a shack, in the dark, because he said, "In these days nobody can recognise true beauty."

A rare treasure was concealed inside a half-abandoned hut, hidden from sight.

Then the bowl suddenly fell, shattering onto the ground.

Joséphine

Here is my story that I'm writing on the spot.

My name is Joséphine. I was born of a French mother, but I lived most of my youth in Italy, my father's homeland, and the country where my parents met and fell in love.

When I was growing up, there were just three of us: my mother, my father and myself. My dad was an ordinary but good looking man who my mother had fallen in love with, a few years before I was born. My mother's family were rich bourgeois, living in the north of France, and my mother run away from them when she was in her early twenties. She never went back, as far as I know, at least while she was with us. Anyway, I personally had never met her relatives, at that time.

She owned, though, a good amount of money, and with the money my father earned from his fish shop, we had a nice lifestyle. I remember a pleasant life, and I thought we were happy. My mother was lovely, very caring, and we spent lot of time together while dad was at work.

However, I also remember a period of time, when Mother tried to seem fine but clearly was not. Alone in her room, she would sit, face in hands, crying. I could see her from the small gap in the doorway, but I was too afraid to ask why she so sad. I was terrified of the idea of losing her. I knew she felt lonely; she didn't have anyone except Dad and me.

Soon, she started to meet new people, and often went out alone. Then my parents fought. In the evenings, when my father came back from his job, they would scream at each other, and Mother would run to her room, crying.

During that period, I was desperately sad, but the worst feeling of all was the powerlessness; I knew I couldn't do anything to change our situation.

Then the day I feared the most came: Mother abandoned us. I was fifteen at the time. I heard a rumour that she was on holiday with her new friends, sipping an aperitif in Naples's harbour, when she met a sailor and left with him.

My father was furious, he stopped talking for a few months, even with me, but I knew he was worried for her. Few months later, a postcard came, addressed to me.

"My sweet dove, I am sorry I had to leave you. I cannot come back to a life that made me an ugly human being. I love life and I want to honour it as much as I can. I hope you will be able to do the same with your own life. You are in my heart, always. It was not easy for me to leave you. Please remember this.

With all my love, your mum."

It was an awful time, and I distinctly recall wondering how people could so easily leave their beloved ones behind.

Anyway, our life, my father's and mine, carried on. We had sorrowful moments, and I sometimes sensed he was angry with me, perhaps because I reminded him of my mother. We had never been close in the past, and after Mother left, our communication worsened.

Two years passed with no change to our life.

Then one day, as often happened, I was sitting in my father's fish shop, reading a book by the side of the counter, when Don Diego came in.

Don Diego was a well-known playboy Mafioso, in our city of Syracuse, and patronised my father's shop at least three times a week. He was constant and punctual, but if the fish was not fresh, there was serious trouble.

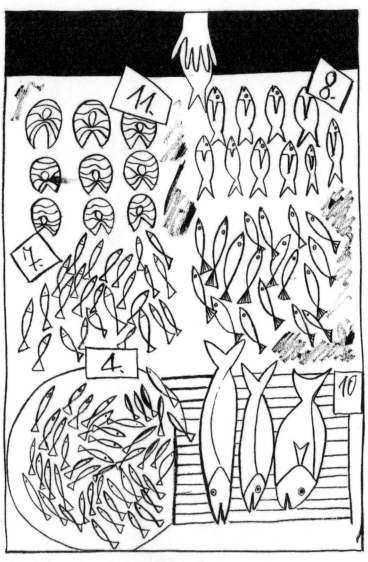

My father often dealt with this shady man for marginal affairs; however, he had never suffered because he always kept a special eye on Mr Diego. In any case, it was on this day that Don Diego laid eyes on me, and I stepped out onto the stage – on a spring morning, giving its first signs of rebirth, the sun's rays beginning to warm the skin, still cold and drained by the winter, and a beautiful scented fragrance of future and beauty hanging in the air.

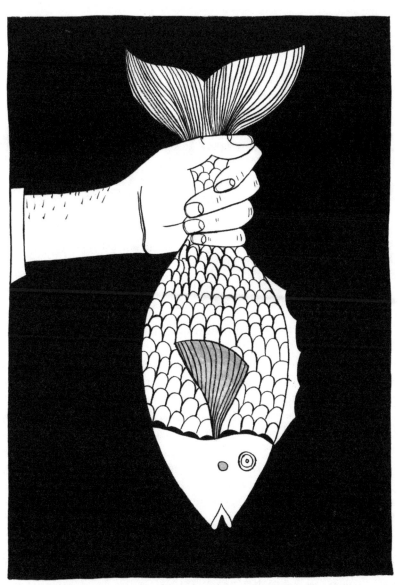

I don't believe Don Diego had even noticed me before, but now, making his day's request to my father, he suddenly showed interested, asking questions about the book I was reading, while trying to conceal a mocking smile. Like a good girl being examined by a teacher, I was polite and replied. A few months later, I found myself entangled in a marriage to the head of the mafia clan of our city.

At the time, I was honoured to have such an important husband. It was surprising to have such a big man interested in me – me who was nothing at all. I do not remember much about the wedding, except that I smiled a lot, and greeted everyone without saying a word, as my groom spoke on my behalf.

The guests on my side were very few; I could count them on one hand, as Dad, coming from another city, did not have many friends in Syracuse. There was Mrs Battistina, our neighbour who used to look after me when I was a kid and my mum had gone; and Mr John, my dad's business partner. On the other side, Don Diego's guests were over one hundred, many of whom I had never seen before.

After the wedding, Don Diego brought me to his beautiful home, where Camilla, my personal maid, prepared me for my first night with my husband. She washed me properly, as I was exhausted and drunk, because of the long day, and I think I had only touched a bit of baked lasagne and a little piece of bridal cake. Before putting me to bed, she spread a teaspoon of acacia honey between my legs, because my husband had ordered her to do so, and she made me wear one of my new, white linen nightdresses, a bit transparent – one we had bought together for my new wardrobe.

Over time, Camilla continued to help me wash, dress, comb my hair, and shop for new clothes, fitting of my new status. She helped me choose all my new notebooks, where I could write my stories and thoughts, without anyone caring about it. I really liked this and it made me feel important.

I knew the mafia existed, but it was like a diaphanous mass, a grey, sticky cloud floating above everyone's heads, untouchable.

The mafia was there but it was not visible. To tell the truth I do not even know if my dad paid a bribe or not, as he did not make me part of his businesses, and I did not tell him the things that went through my head.

What I did not know was that Don Diego, who was known to be obsessed with personal power, was said to have shot his first wife in the forehead, when she failed to give him an heir. While she died in her own blood, he left the house, in the middle of the night, to get a drink. No one dared to ask him how he avoided jail.

I thought I was in love. Even though Don Diego was past his fifties, he was still a powerful, tall and strong man, with brusque manners and a rough moustache that left me with burning red lips after we made love.

I was giving myself to him as I would not have thought I could. I was a little wild creature enjoying pleasure, sucking, touching, sometimes slow, other times with eagerness, and he liked this very much.

He also liked the fact that I looked much younger than I was, more than thirty years younger than him. He told me this excited him. And seeing him excited, made me excited too. In short, I must say that, the beginning our marriage was at least interesting from the physical point of view. Don Diego helped me to open a crack into the world of pleasure.

I fell pregnant a few months after the wedding, and he treated me like the perfect wife, especially after the birth of our first child, Giorgio, who was the light of his eyes. Don Diego saw Giorgio as heir to the empire he had built, since the death of his own father, from whom he had taken the reins of the family business – lemons and oranges, as far as I knew.

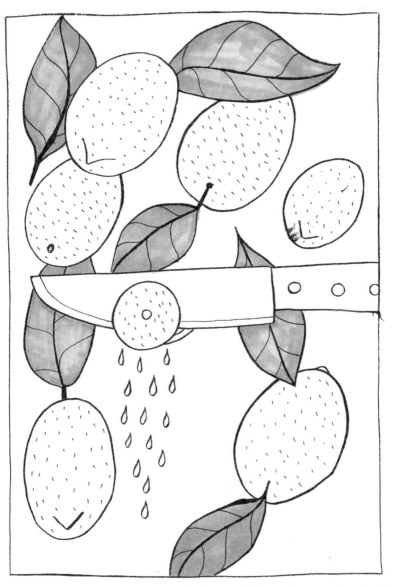

After Giorgio, Amalia was born, and then Flora – a little girl who, unlike her siblings, caused me much less suffering during labour – perhaps because she was the third.

She was tiny, delicate and beautiful, the cutest among all. Not that the others were not lovely. In fact, as the proverb says, self-praise is not praise, and all my children were, of course, exquisite to me.

Giorgio was a duplicate of his father. Seeing them together was like having a journey through time: they had the same mannerisms while eating; if someone was speaking, they were interrupting the conversation in exactly the same way, because it was obvious they had something to say so urgently they couldn't bear to hold back, even for a second; and they walked and moved as if they were the one person.

Amalia was a perfect mix of my and Don Diego's genes, and this gave her a huge degree of independence from the family. She was a polite and good girl, graceful and silent. From the age of four she was able to read, so spent much of her time alone in her room with her nose on a book.

On the other hand, Flora was very much like me, and even like my mum, as much as I remembered her: all three of us had a thick mane of long red hair, fair skin, white as milk, which freckled with every ray of sunshine that intruded under the sunshade, and delicate features with lustrous, full lips.

GRANDMA   JOSEPHINE   FLORA

Flora was like an erupting volcano; she couldn't stand still. From birth, she showed a great will, and insisted on enrolling in a dance course when she was only three years old. Her father, who usually didn't care much about his own children, except of course for Giorgio, his favourite, admitted he admired Flora for her tenacity and her unstoppable energy.

34

Dance shaped Flora's growing body, perfected her posture, and channelled her enormous energy. It allowed her to become a beautiful wild flower, abandoning our home from the age of ten to study at the École de danse de l'Opéra national de Paris.

During those years, when my children were growing, in search of their personality and vocation, I also grew up in my own way. After all, I was only seventeen when I got married, and I still did not know anything about myself, or the wider world. The notebooks I had bought in the city centre, since the beginning of my marriage, were aligning by date on the shelves of my studio, and I wrote every day: stories, a personal diary, poetry and novels. Everything remained on the shelves of my room, lined up by typology, in chronological order. Writing was the thing I liked the most in the world, and I was immensely happy when Amalia, at the age of ten, appeared on a sultry summer afternoon, with a happy shy smile, bringing me the first book she had written. She was looking a little bit like me, after all!

My babies were growing fast. I loved them so dearly, but somehow I set them free, to allow them to pursue their dreams, to become adults and the beautiful humans they deserved to be. I wanted them be courageous enough to be individuals, and to make their lives an exquisite piece of art. This was a big step for me, because it meant for them to be free, I might be left behind. But of course this was the right thing to do. I wanted to be their support, anytime they needed me, but I also wanted them to be capable to swim free in the ocean of life.

About Don Diego and me – we stopped having relations, almost right after I gave birth to Flora.

Sadly, after I had accomplished the mission he assigned during the marriage – giving him one or more heirs – he began to ignore me, and for years we did not sleep together. Slowly, I became only a presence in the house – fed, given new clothes to replace old ones, and two rooms of the house for personal use. I still managed the house and took the best care I could of my children. I felt terribly sorry because my son Giorgio and I were not talking at all, even though he was always respectful to me. I knew he loved me, but he had learnt too much from his own father, and he was not able to share his feelings, or show his love to his beloved ones. I should admit that I regret very much I was not able, at that time, to become closer to him, as I was lost in my own thoughts and angry with Diego, who took my child away from me.

While Diego was polite to me, I was treated as if I were an icon, for whom flowers were put on an altar, every third Friday of the month. I existed as a ghost woman, a non-person. Nothing was shared between us. I felt transparent.

But I was a woman in the full bloom of spring, both physically and emotionally. Though I had never loved my husband, being the object of his desires, and the very physicality we had shared, had brought me pleasure, at least in the beginning. Over time, I stopped looking for Don Diego and started to touch myself instead.

At night, immediately after lying on my royal canopy bed, I folded my legs and opened my thighs like a lotus flower. I wetted my index finger in my mouth and gently touched me, while with the other hand I felt my breast, my belly, exploring my entire hot and smooth body, and then increased the rhythm of my caresses, which became more and more profound and violent, until I felt a sense of absolute liberation and satisfaction. But I needed more warmth; I wanted to love and be loved.

My studio overlooked our villa's garden. One day, as I looked out of the window, contemplating the spring air of a mid-March afternoon, I stretched out over the window sill and asked myself, "Is life only this, really?" In my heart, I was very sad, and I wondered if there really was something worth living for. My books, my writings, were not enough anymore. My diaries had become collections of blood, dropping from my heart, and nothing else. I needed to feel life inside me, again.

Suddenly, I understood that the questions one asks herself are like powerful spells, capable of cracking daily reality in the blink of an eye. My life, as I knew it, was now wrecked, but later it would be reassembled into a more beautiful, exquisite art piece, taking a shape somehow closer to the true essence of my own spirit.

The garden blossoms again

A few days later, the first amazing thing happened. My husband decided our garden needed to be restored, and he called an army of gardeners to prune the trees that had overgrown, plant new flowers in the flowerbeds, redraw the garden paths of rounded flat stones, and to create a new and more enjoyable space with benches, gazebos, climbing plants and tropical fruit trees. This would allow us to fully enjoy the outdoor spaces of the house.

Well, as one of the most ordinary clichés that ever existed, I fell in love with one of the gardeners, Fabrizio.

But I must first add that my situation, in spite of the freedom I had in my domestic life, was in fact an imprisonment: I couldn't go out except on Sundays, when I went to Church with the rest of the family. Our villa was few miles from the centre, and I could go to town to buy what I needed, such as clothes, notebooks, books or things for the kids, but only if Camilla, my faithful maid, was accompanying me, and only on those mornings when Don Diego also went to Syracuse and met me in the city centre.

I was choking. Trapped.

40

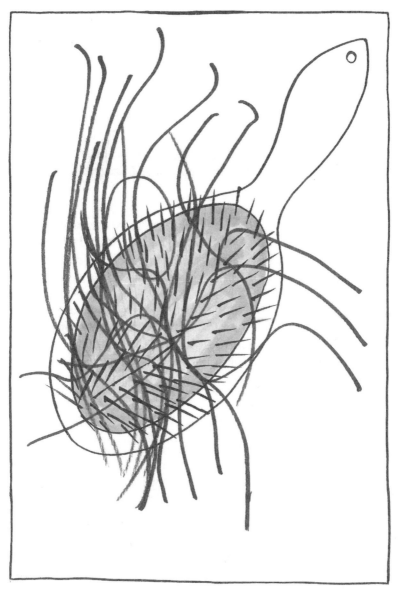

My hair started to fall out, strands remaining in the brush when Camilla combed and prepared my tresses for the day. I lost my appetite and my weight dropped drastically. Worse, I lost the urge to write and invent stories. I was pinched and depressed. So, it was something like an act of magic when Diego had the brilliant idea of restoring the garden. It was as if I had somehow led the spirits of life to give me a gift, to fulfil one of my desires.

41

When the gardeners started work, I was wearing an old pair of high-waisted pants and a man's blue shirt, perfectly ironed by expert hands. I jumped in to help, thinking that healthy exercise would improve my mood.

While I worked – my hands in the humid soil, my nails black with grounds and little stones – I thought about nothing. My head emptied, and I started to relax, all the accumulated tension from my unhappiness, leaving my body. I accepted the void in me, and I felt lighter and freer.

Those mornings in the open air also restored my appetite, so much so that I returned to the house ravenous and not wanting to wait for my meals even one extra minute. I had never experienced such impatience for food, even in my adolescence.

For years, at the beginning of the warm season, our family would eat outside on a raw wooden table covered with a snow-white tablecloth and laden with white porcelain picnic plates decorated with a simple blue border, and light blue transparent glasses for wine and water.

It was just after one of these open-air lunches that I started talking to Fabrizio. Everyone, including my husband, had finished their coffee and retired to their afternoon siesta.

Fabrizio asked me if I liked the flowers we were planting. I replied that my husband had chosen them all, except for the light pink peonies, which were my favourite, and that I had stubbornly insisted on placing the two large bushes at the sides of the stone path we were remaking. I would have also liked to plant some beautiful red and yellow chrysanthemums, but my husband forbade that because he thought they were lugubrious flowers, beautiful only at the graveyard, so I planted some of them on the terrace of my studio.

Fabrizio told me the peonies were very beautiful. "Unusual flowers," he added, smiling. That was enough for me to fall in love with him. I was in my early thirties, but emotionally I was still a little girl. And now, even after many years, I realise love does not need a rational reason to blossom. In my eyes, Fabrizio represented what I wanted to be: a free person, someone who didn't need to answer to anyone but himself.

I remember that period as one of the most beautiful times in my life. The first time we kissed, it was late at night. I made sure everyone in the house was asleep, and I went downstairs, like a ghost, noiseless, ethereal and wrapped in a light dressing gown that swung and opened a little between my legs, as I hurried down the stairs to the garden.

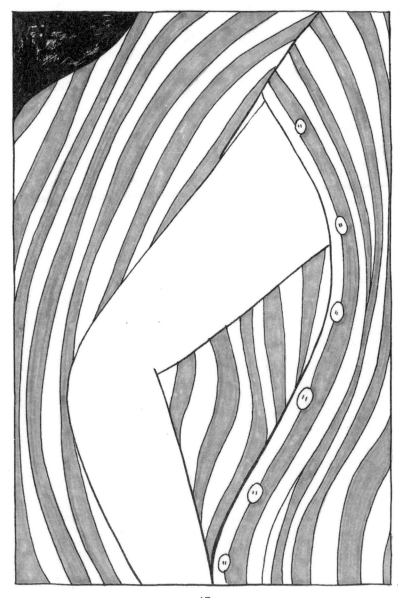

Fabrizio was waiting for me near a centennial olive tree, a spot of the garden visible only from the living room windows. His smooth, warm skin smelled like jasmine and vanilla. We

kissed for hours – he biting my lips, sneaking his big delicate hands between my legs, and I almost fainting with pleasure. But we had to be careful: Don Diego was not a man to be trifled with.

So Fabrizio left each time, shortly before dawn, and returned a few hours later, to work in the garden. For several mornings, after our night-time meetings, I got up very late, not used to staying awake during the night.

Everything, compared to my feelings for Fabrizio, was nothing. Unreal. Insignificant.

The mornings we worked in the garden, I had to be careful not to pay too much attention to Fabrizio, in case my husband suspected something. The scariest thing was that, to me, it was so obvious how much I liked him: I blushed every time he talked to me, even in presence of other people. I thought about him constantly, and I found it incredible that others didn't notice. My mood shifted, my heart exploding with love, and sometimes I felt as if I was walking on clouds. When we met alone, in the nights, we talked and laughed, and it was so nice to feel that someone actually cared about me, as much as he did.

But it couldn't last, and after a few months, we decided to stop seeing each other. It had become too dangerous for both of us, especially when one of the gardeners said something to Fabrizio about us, and he became frozen with fear. I was still sure Diego didn't suspect anything yet, but being sure was not enough. Even if just one gardener was suspicious, we knew we shouldn't take any further risks.

A few days later, Fabrizio told me he would leave Sicily for a while. After that, he didn't come to work at the garden anymore. The only person I could ever trust about this topic was another of the gardeners, Luigi, Fabrizio's best friend. I decided to approach him, to ask if he knew anything about Fabrizio's whereabouts. He said they had gone together to Palermo, where Fabrizo had taken a ship and left the island. I didn't ask anything else. I was just so relieved, and I hoped inside my heart that what Luigi told me was the truth, and not just something he'd made up for me not to worry.

I realised that I could no longer stay in the house of Don Diego, and I started to think about escaping. I knew for sure my husband's reputation and pride would never let him accept me leaving him for another man, or leaving him to be by myself. I thought about Don Diego's first wife – the ugly end she had met. But the thing most important to me was to get away from my imprisonment, and to be as far away as possible from the man I married.

I decided I had to take my time. I could not hasten things because the success of the plan was at stake. I carved into my memory the image of Evelina, Don Diego's first wife, dead and immersed in a pool of her own blood.

Organising my project lasted more than a year. I put aside a small amount of housekeeping money each week, wrapping it in a towel in my lingerie drawer. I prepared a small suitcase in which I neatly organised comfortable clothes – no luxurious dresses or corsages, but wide cotton or linen shirts, and large skirts that would not cling to my hips.

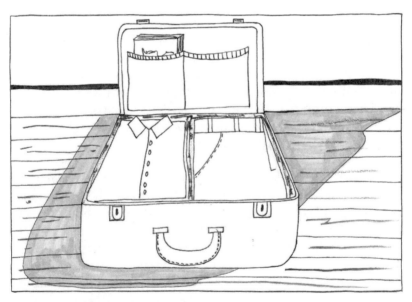

In one of my husband's newspapers, I found a telephone number for a ship travelling to Spain, and I booked a ticket. I would travel from Palermo, to Barcelona, then on to Brest, France, where I had relatives, or at least I hoped there would be someone who knew my mother in the past.

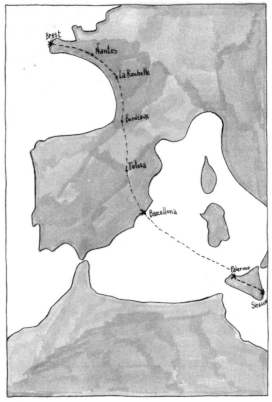

49

I planned everything for that one day. It was a chance I would not get again, for a long time at least. Diego had left for Rome, to visit his mother for a few days. She was always calling him to visit her, since she didn't want to come back to Sicily after her husband had died. But Diego usually refused, saying he didn't have time to go. Now was the perfect time for me to arrange my departure. If I was lucky, Diego wouldn't find out I was gone until the day after. Everything else, I left in the hands of fate.

Everything was ready. The ship that would take me to Barcelona was arriving that night. It was time to face everything. In the afternoon, I burnt all my old diaries and books: I didn't want anything of me left in the house. I grabbed the kitchen scissors, and with a few snips, cut off my long hair. My tresses fell into the sink, where I easily cleaned them away, leaving no traces behind me.

Giorgio was sleeping. I wished I could have told him and my daughters about my departure, but I could guess what Don Diego's reaction would be and didn't want to risk their lives. So, I left, without saying anything. This is the biggest regret of my whole life. I know exactly what it feels like to be abandoned by your mother, but I couldn't break the circle both my mother and I had been trapped in.

Dressed in my husband's trousers and shirt, I grabbed my suitcase, money, and ran. Luigi waited for me a few curves from the home gate. Disguised in a hood, he drove me to Palermo, both of us fearful that someone would stop us, or worse, recognise us.

It was August 15th, and the church bell rang two strokes in muffle tones. At the port, he pushed a small crinkled piece of paper into my hand. Only later did I realise it was Fabrizio's telephone number.

Many days have passed since that night. The truth for me is that, when you begin to live your life in a manner worthy of your true, enormous and limitless spirit, what you have been through, in your past, does not weigh on your shoulders like the burden of lost time, but rather it is perceived as a journey, or a necessary stage of life, to reach where you are today.

Kinsugi

Few years ago, on one of my voyages, I discovered a technique for repairing broken objects, without hiding their past. It's a Japanese art called Kinsugi. I used this method to mend a beautiful soup tureen, which I'd found in a shack. I placed the tureen in my studio, on the shelves alongside my new books.

I look at it every day, and so I recall the infinite and the stars of the universe, which I am also part of, and from whom, in a one way or another, I also come from.

Postscript: A letter from Virginia Woolf

I imagined receiving a letter from Virginia Woolf, a writer I deeply love and who I've learned to appreciate more and more over time, having read many of her books and published diaries. I would like to report here a part of the letter, because the letter I imagined she would write to me would be about looking for freedom in life, and about working to bring to light our own uniqueness, without constantly trying to be like others.

Dear Virginia,

Already your name is almost flattering me, even though I'm probably not the only reason for this case of homonymy.

It seems that you are starting to like me more and more: I know well that sometimes it takes time to really connect.

But let's get to the point: you write asking me suggestions about how to become a successful writer, and of course I don't have any.

What I personally did during my life was just trying to follow my own being, even to the bones, which, to me, meant to write. The only thing I can tell you, the only good advice I can possibly give you, is to always look for the part of you that represents your most precious and most hidden diamond.
Keep everything clear in your mind, so that all your actions

serve to bring to light, like a rag cleaning dusty furniture, your uniqueness, and do not search for what makes you similar to others. Surround yourself with people who understand this need, which is not just yours, but everyone's. Only the luckiest ones realise it in time.

Everything you write, and all your other interests, are a glimpse into a beautiful sky, and you can open the gap a little more each time, if what you do comes from the desire of your inner self.

Thank you for writing me. This new connection between dimensions is very good news!

I think of you and I am ready to help you, if you need,

V.W.